Beany and the
Dreaded Wedding

Thanks to:

The students of Brecknock School, Governor Mifflin School District, especially Jessica Freese, for their great spelling bee suggestions.

Nancy Liebert, for orchestrating "Project Flower Girl Memory Input."

And a stupendous thank-you to flower girl Laura Blaylock, whose picture, smiling at me from my writing table, inspired me throughout the writing of this book.

Beany
and the Dreaded Wedding

Susan Wojciechowski

illustrated by
Susanna Natti

CANDLEWICK PRESS

For my precious daughter, Mary,
who was, is, and always will be
the real Beany
S. W.
★
To Deanie, with love
S. N.

Text copyright © 2000 by Susan Wojciechowski
Illustrations copyright © 2000 by Susanna Natti

Library of Congress Cataloging-in-Publication Data
Wojciechowski, Susan.
Beany and the dreaded wedding / Susan Wojciechowski ;
illustrated by Susanna Natti.—1st ed.
p. cm.
Summary: Beany loves her cousin Amy but is worried
about something going wrong if she agrees to be
the flower girl in Amy's wedding.
ISBN 0-7636-0924-2
[1. Weddings—Fiction. 2. Cousins—Fiction.]
I. Natti, Susanna, ill. II. Title.
PZ7.W8183 Bc2000
[Fic]—dc21 99-052343

2 4 6 8 10 9 7 5 3 1

Printed in the United States of America

This book was typeset in Bembo.
The illustrations were done in pen and ink.

Candlewick Press
2067 Massachusetts Avenue
Cambridge, Massachusetts 02140

Contents

★ ★ ★
★ ★ ★

The Decision

It was the first day of summer vacation. Carol Ann and I were in my back yard building a tuffet under the maple tree when my big brother, Philip, came to the door and yelled, "Beanhead, there's a phone call for you." My real name is Bernice Lorraine Sherwin-Hendricks, but most people call me Beany, except for my brother. Sometimes he calls me Beanhead and I don't like it, not one bit.

I wiped my hands down the sides of my

shorts to get the dirt off as I walked across the yard.

"What the heck is that?" Philip asked, sitting down on the porch steps.

"It's a tuffet," I answered.

"It looks like a pile of dirt."

"We're going to pack it down with a shovel and put grass seed all over it and pretty soon it will be a tuffet," I said. "After that we'll sit on it to eat curds and whey or read."

"It looks dumb," said my brother.

"You look dumb," answered Carol Ann. She is very brave. I would never in a million years say that to my brother, but my best friend, Carol Ann, always says whatever she's thinking. Sometimes I like it, like today. But sometimes I wish she wouldn't, like the day I wore a pair of barrettes to school with long ribbons hanging down from them that I got from my cousin Amy. When Amy graduated from college and moved to New York City to learn how to be a lawyer, she cleaned out her bedroom and gave me everything she didn't want. The barrettes were in a big box full of old shoes, purses, jewelry, and other neat stuff. When I wore the barrettes, Carol Ann told me I looked like I had spaghetti hanging from my head. She told me just as I was going to the front of our classroom to lead the pledge of allegiance, so I couldn't even take them out. All I could do was lead the pledge with my head hanging down, hoping no one would notice the spaghetti barrettes. Then my teacher asked me if there was something wrong with my neck and sent me to the school nurse, all because of Carol Ann.

When Carol Ann called my brother dumb, I wondered what he would do. He's thirteen so he could do plenty, but he just ignored her and told me to make my call short because he wanted to use the phone.

I picked up the phone in the kitchen.

"Hello?"

"Hi, Bean," said the voice at the other end of the line. It was my cousin Amy, the one who moved to New York City. She's lucky. She lives in an apartment with her very

own fire escape out the bedroom window.

"Hi," I said. "Are you out on your fire escape?"

"No, I'm here in town, visiting my parents for a few days, and I called to see if you're free this afternoon. There's something special I want to ask you," Amy said. I got so excited I smiled right into the receiver. Amy is one of my most favorite people in the whole world. She lived right around the corner from me for my whole life until she left home to go to college. When she lived at home, she was my baby sitter. She brought me caramel popcorn whenever she baby-sat. Now I hardly ever get to see her, especially since she got engaged. Amy and her New York boyfriend told the whole family at Easter dinner that they were getting married. Now they're always busy getting ready for the wedding.

"I'm free right now," I said.

"I'll be right over," answered Amy.

I ran into the yard and told Carol Ann she'd have to leave. Then I ran upstairs to wash the tuffet dirt off my hands and put on the gold chain with a heart hanging from it that Amy gave me last Christmas. In a few minutes I heard her coming up my front porch steps, calling out, "Hi, people!" Mom and I came outside and we all hugged. Amy gave me a big plastic tub of caramel popcorn, then sat down on the porch swing. She was wearing jean shorts and a T-shirt, just like I was. That made me feel good, just like I feel when people tell me I look like her. We both have short hair that sometimes sticks out in weird ways if we sleep on it wrong, and we both have freckles that we're always complaining about.

"How are the wedding plans coming?" Mom asked Amy.

"Hectic," said Amy. "You know how my mom is. She comes up with some new idea every day."

"Well, if there's anything I can do to help, just yell," said Mom, as she left to go to an exercise class at the Y.

While Amy and I ate popcorn, she asked me what was new, so I told her about the end of school and about how I'm busy trying to talk my parents out of sending me to overnight camp this summer.

"They're making me go and I know I'll hate it."

"You might not," said Amy. "I thought I'd hate camp the first time I went, but after a couple of days I started to like it."

"Well, I know I won't, and I don't, don't, don't want to go. Hey, would you tell my mom and dad not to make me go? They'd listen to you."

"Sure I will, if you pay me a thousand dollars." Amy laughed. Then she said, "No, seriously, I know you'll end up liking camp. If it'll help, I'll write to you every day while you're there. Now, fill me in on what else you're doing."

"I got a sewing badge in Scouts. We had to sew skirts," I told her. "Mine came out all wrinkly, and when I put it on, it was so tight I couldn't walk very well. But that's okay because the badge was for making the skirt, not wearing it."

"What else are you up to?" Amy asked.

"Carol Ann and I are building a tuffet," I said.

"For Scouts?" she asked.

"No, for sitting on."

"Cool!" my cousin said. "Can I see it?" We went into the back yard. I was a little mad to see that Carol Ann had not gone

home like I asked her to. She was by the
side of the garage, shoveling dirt into a wheel-
barrow to use on our tuffet.

"Hi," she said to Amy. "Did Beany tell
you what we're doing? I got this great idea
to build a tuffet."

"I know all about it," Amy answered. She

sat down under the maple tree and patted the ground next to her for me to sit down, too. I sat close to her so my arm touched hers. She told me my tuffet was the nicest one she had ever seen in real life. She put her arm around me.

"Remember when I used to baby-sit you and we'd sit under this tree?"

"Yeah," I said. "You read Dr. Seuss books to me while I ate caramel popcorn."

"I like Dr. Seuss," called Carol Ann from the side of the garage.

"And do you remember how you used to love the game Hungry Hungry Hippos?" Amy asked me.

"I used to like that game, too," Carol Ann called out.

I wrinkled my nose up at Carol Ann to let her know she was bothering me, but she turned around and didn't see it.

"Every time you came over," I reminded Amy, "I made you play it with me a kajillion times."

Amy groaned. "You were such a monster."

"I was?"

"No, I'm just kidding. You were the sweetest, Bean, and you still are. If I ever have a daughter, I want her to be just like you."

From the garage I heard Carol Ann snort, but I ignored her. I told Amy I wished she didn't have to live in New York, even if she did have a cool fire escape.

"Yeah, I know," said Amy. "But look at it this way. If I didn't live in New York, I never would have met my hunk-a-love, which brings me to the reason I came over here, Bean. It's about the wedding."

Carol Ann stopped shoveling and yelled out, "I love weddings."

"The big day is going to be in November," Amy went on, ignoring Carol Ann, "and I want to ask you something very important." She took both my hands and squeezed them so tight I almost yelled "ouch" but I scrunched up my face and kept quiet.

"Peter and I want you to be in our wedding. You'd be the flower girl and the ring bearer together," she said. Then she put one of her hands over my mouth. "Don't answer

now. Just think about it and I'll call you tomorrow for your decision. Okay?"

My hands started to shake. My legs felt like Jell-O. "Okay," I said. We went into the house, with Amy talking the whole time about her hunk-a-love and the wedding.

"Well, I've got to scoot," Amy said. "I'm only home for a few days and my mom wants to work on wedding plans with me. Oh, one more thing before I go—could you hold open the third weekend in August for Ladies' Day? I'm planning a trip home especially for that." Ladies' Day is what Amy calls the day she takes me to Crystal Lake Amusement Park every summer. I love Ladies' Day. Amy lets me pick all the rides for us to go on and I get to eat all the cotton candy I want.

The minute Amy left, Carol Ann came running out of the yard, yelling, "Beany, you're finally going to be in a wedding!" She made it sound like she'd been waiting a million years for me to be in one. "You'll have so much fun. It's a known fact that people in the wedding party have the most fun of anyone. I was a flower girl once and it was the best day of my life. I got to walk down the aisle of the church with everyone looking at me. Then I stood at the altar. I got to have my picture taken with the bride and groom,

and I sat at a long table with them for dinner. After that I danced with the grownups all afternoon."

I didn't tell Carol Ann, but those were the exact reasons I *didn't* want to be in my cousin's wedding. What if the back of my hair came out all weird and lumpy that day and everyone could see it while I stood at the altar? What if the photographer asked us to say "cheeseburger" while he took the picture, and snapped it right while I was on the *b* sound? What if I dribbled soup or had a piece of food hanging on my chin while I ate? What if they made me do the chicken dance? Scariest of all, though, was the thought of walking down the aisle with everyone looking at me. I didn't know if I could do that.

"I have a great idea!" Carol Ann said. "Julie from school was in a wedding and I've been in a wedding. I'm going to start a

Flower Girl Club and I might invite you to join. At the meetings we'll talk about the weddings and show each other pictures. It'll be so fun!" Carol Ann talked like being in a wedding wasn't even something a person had to think over and maybe say no. She talked like my decision was already made, which it wasn't. She talked like there wasn't anything to be scared of or worried about.

I asked Carol Ann if she'd mind stopping work on the tuffet till the next day. Then I went upstairs and lay on my bed, holding my stuffed moose, Jingle Bell. I told him all the things I was worried about, especially the part about walking down the aisle with everyone looking at me. I told him I didn't think I could do it. Jingle Bell understood.

That night, when my dad came into my room to read to me, I asked him how many steps it takes to walk down the whole aisle of a church.

"I don't know," he said. "It depends on the church. Why?"

"Well, I haven't told anyone about this yet because I don't know if I'm going to do it, but Amy asked me to be in her wedding.

I'm a little scared about walking down the aisle."

"I would be, too," my dad answered. "But have you thought about what it means to be in the wedding?"

"No, I was using up all my brain thinking about everything that could go wrong. What does it mean?"

"It means your cousin loves you so much

she wants you to share in one of the most important days of her life. It means you're pretty special to her." Dad kissed me, turned out my light, and closed the bedroom door just the way I like it, letting a little crack of light come in from the hall.

"Did you hear that, Jingle Bell? I'm special." I hugged my moose and fell asleep.

The next day Amy called me back. "Well, Bean, will you do it? Will you be in my wedding?"

"Yes," I said.

"Yahoo, the Bean said yes!" yelled Amy, so loud I bet everyone in her house could hear her. After I hung up the phone I stood in the kitchen smiling. Philip came by and told me I looked dumb. But I couldn't help it. I just smiled and smiled till my cheeks started to hurt.

I decided I would make Amy proud that

she had picked me. I would do everything exactly right. I would walk down that aisle even if it was one mile long, even if there were a million people there, all looking at me. I decided I would be a better flower girl than even Carol Ann was. In fact, I would be the best flower girl in the whole world.

The Wedding Gift

★ ★ ★ ★ ★

The wedding wasn't until November, so I tried not to worry about it too much over the summer. I had enough summer stuff to worry about. My biggest problem was camp. My parents signed me up to go in August, so I spent all of July thinking up ways to get out of going. No luck. My mom and dad forced me to go. Amy was right about camp; it started out scary and ended up fun. I might even go again next summer.

Right after camp I started worrying about the first day of school. One afternoon I was sitting on the front porch swing, laying out all my new school supplies: Snoopy pencil sharpener, box of crayons, ruler, pack of tissues, Hello Kitty pencils, cherry-scented eraser. Philip came out and laughed at me. He said I was the only kid on the planet who liked going back to school. He was wrong. I don't like going back to school; I just like to be prepared. I was testing my markers to make sure they all worked when my mother came out and sat down next to me with a big stack of mail-order catalogs.

"What are you doing?" I asked.

"I'm checking to see if any of these catalogs have the wedding gifts Amy and Peter registered for," she answered.

"What's registering?" I asked.

"It's like making a giant wish list. Amy and Peter went into a department store and picked out the dishes, glassware, silverware, towels, sheets, blankets, and whatever else

they'd like to own when they get married. All their choices got typed into a computer. That's called registering. Amy gave me a copy of the computer list, and I'm trying to find their dishes in these catalogs. Sometimes I can get things cheaper in catalogs than in stores."

I looked at the list. It was three pages long, almost as long as my brother's birthday wish list last year. I picked up a catalog from Mom's pile and tried to find the pattern of Amy and Peter's glasses.

"Here it is! The pattern called Skylark!" I yelled. I traced my finger down to the price list. "What? Twenty dollars for one glass? You better call the catalog and tell them they made a mistake. They probably meant to write two dollars instead of twenty."

"It's no mistake," said Mom. "Those glasses are made of crystal. We don't have any in this house because if we did, you or Philip would probably break some of them, and then we'd have to sell you in order to buy replacements."

I looked at the picture of the Skylark glasses. The part you held was long and thin, and the drinking part was on top of that.

Each glass had little cuts all over it, and the holding part was shaped like a twirled licorice stick. I decided I wanted to buy two glasses for them, just from me. I could picture Amy and her hunk-a-love sitting at their dining

room table with candles on it, clinking their glasses and smiling at each other and saying, "Isn't Beany the greatest flower girl in the whole universe? That girl is not cheap."

The only problem was I didn't have forty

dollars. I didn't even have four dollars. I had spent all my money on a round, flower-printed pillow that I saw at Kmart and had to have because it would look perfect on my tuffet.

"Why can't we be rich?" I said to my mother. "Why can't Dad be a bank president like Julie's father, instead of being a dumb old computer guy?"

Julie's family is so rich they have a candy dish of M&M's in their living room all the time. Once I asked Julie if anybody can just take M&M's whenever they feel like it, or did Julie's mom warn her that they are just for company, and if she so much as touches them she will never see another M&M in the house as long as she lives. Julie told me she can take M&M's anytime she wants, so when I'm at her house I open my fingers as wide as they'll go and scoop up a handful. I put them in my pocket and try to make them last for the rest of the day. When I eat supper at Julie's house I am super careful to mind my manners. They use cloth napkins, so I never wipe my mouth. I don't want to get the napkin dirty. And when her mom offers me seconds on pork chops or apple-sauce, I always say "I thank you" instead of just plain "thank you." My Great Aunt Kay told me once that rich people say it that way.

Whenever I leave their house, I wonder what it would be like to change places with Julie for even a day. She would not want to be me for a day, though. She'd get called Beanhead by my brother and have to use the paper napkins my mother buys in packages of two hundred because they're cheaper that way. The next day Julie would probably blab to the whole school that we don't even have M&M's at our house.

I asked my mom if I could have the catalog page with the picture of the Skylark glasses. After I put all my school stuff in my backpack, I went to my room and tacked the page on my bulletin board. Then Jingle Bell and I lay on my bed trying to figure out how I could pay for two glasses.

The next day I called Carol Ann to ask if she had any ideas about how I could get some money, lots of money.

"What for?"

"Wedding present."

"Oh, you'll definitely need lots," she said. "It's a known fact that the people who are in a wedding have to give the best presents of anyone. And if you don't, everyone will talk about you. When I was a flower girl, I gave a silver bowl. It was made of real silver plate." I didn't know if I should believe Carol Ann or not. She tells me lots of known facts that

turn out to be wrong. Sometimes she acts like she knows everything there is to know, just because she's four months older than me, but she doesn't. She does not know how to spell *deodorant,* which caused her to lose our classroom spelling bee last week. She spelled it *deodorent.* I know it was not nice of me, but when she lost, I was a little bit glad.

Carol Ann is my best friend because we live on the same street and sit next to each other on the school bus, but sometimes I don't really like her that much.

It was quiet on the other end of the phone while Carol Ann tried to think of a money-raising idea. Then she said, "Okay, here's what we'll do. We'll set up a table on your front lawn and sell lemonade and Rice Krispie Treats. There is not a person on Earth who can walk by Rice Krispie Treats without wanting one. We'll make tons of money." I didn't like the way Carol Ann kept saying "we." But she did have a great idea.

When I told my mom Carol Ann's idea, she didn't think it was so great. "Beany, you'll have to buy all the ingredients," she said. "You could end up losing money. Think about it." I went out on the porch and watched a squirrel running along the

branches of our maple tree for a couple of minutes. Then I went into the kitchen and told my mother I still wanted to do it. "If you lend me the money to buy the stuff I need, I'll pay you back from the money I make," I promised.

I made the first batch of Treats the next day. Spreading the stuff into a pan was the hardest part. It kept sticking to my fingers, and I couldn't make it stretch into the corners like my mother does when she makes Rice Krispie Treats for our school bake sales. While I was doing the Treats, Carol Ann mixed up some lemonade from a can of powdered mix. Then Mom cut the squares while I made a sign with colored markers and a big piece of cardboard.

Rice Krispie Treats
50 cents
Lemonade 50 cents

When she saw the sign, Carol Ann took a marker and wrote *tasty* in front of Rice Krispie Treats and *ice cold* in front of lemonade. Then she dumped a tray of ice cubes into the lemonade, and we set everything up on a folding table on the front lawn.

"Get ready to make some money," Carol Ann said as we sat down in two folding

chairs behind the table. While we waited for customers, Carol Ann pulled a book out of her backpack. "Look," she said. "I found this in my sister Margo's room. It's a book full of interesting but weird facts." Carol Ann flipped the pages and read out loud a list of weird things wrong with people. There was a man who couldn't stop eating silverware, and a person whose hands did opposite things, like if his left hand smoothed his hair down, his right hand would mess it up. Or if his left hand zipped his pants, his right hand would unzip them. Carol Ann put the book down and we tried to make our hands do opposite things. Carol Ann picked up a Rice Krispie Treat and put it in her mouth with one hand. Then she yanked it out and put it down with her other hand. She kept going on like that till we were laughing so hard we almost fell off our chairs.

Philip came out to find out what we were laughing at, and when we told him, he started doing it, too. Then we took turns reading lists. There was a list of weird inventions like a bed that floats up to the ceiling when no one is in it, and a list of weird facts like: A pig is the only animal besides a human that can get a sunburn. There was even a list of towns that have weird names, like Ding Dong, Texas.

"Excuse me," we heard a voice say, "I'd like to buy a snack." It was our first customer, Mr. Batog from down the street. We had been so busy laughing I hadn't even seen him come up to the table. I never even got to say "May I help you?" like I had practiced the night before in front of a mirror. I jumped to my feet and lifted the sheet of waxed paper off the plate. There were only eight Treats instead of the twenty we started with.

"Where are the rest?" I asked.

"We must have eaten them," Carol Ann said, "while we were reading lists and waiting for customers."

"I think we drank a lot of the lemonade, too," added Philip, as he peered into the pitcher. "All that laughing must have made us thirsty."

Krispie Treats
cents
nade 50 cents

All of a sudden Carol Ann said, "I have to go home," and jumped on her bike. She always does that. When there's trouble, she leaves. Once Carol Ann and her book were gone, Philip left, too.

After I sold Mr. Batog a Krispie Treat, I sat alone watching the sidewalk in each direction, waiting for the chance to say "May I help you?" to the next person who walked by. Without Carol Ann there it got boring. I looked down the street one way, then the other. The only people I saw were my father cutting the lawn and Mikey next door, who got off his Big Wheel and came over to ask if he could have a Rice Krispie Treat.

"Sorry, Mikey, they're not free. But I'll give you one if you'll do me a favor. I have to go to the bathroom. Could you just sit here till I get back? If customers come, tell them I'll be right out. Can you do that?" Mikey shook his head yes.

"Are you going to touch anything?" I asked. Mikey shook his head no. Mikey is only four, and I didn't know if I could trust him, but I had to go to the bathroom bad.

When I came back outside, Mikey was gone. I ran to the table to see if everything was all right. I looked into the pitcher.

There was still some lemonade in it. I lifted the waxed paper and looked at the plate. Seven Treats were there. But something was wrong. The Treats were covered with grass! I screamed. Just then, Mikey's mother came out of their house, pulling Mikey by the hand. Halfway across the driveway he sat down. She had to pick him up and carry him to my yard.

"Mikey has something to tell you," she said.

Mikey sat down on the grass and started to suck his thumb. I put my hands on my hips and wrinkled up my forehead to show him I was very mad. Finally he said, "Doggie do it." Then he ran back into his house before his mother could stop him.

"I was watching out the window," Mikey's mother explained. "You know that huge black dog, Dr. Pepper, from the next

street that runs across the lawns, scaring everyone? Well, it came through your yard while you were in the house. It ran right up to the table and knocked the plate off. I'll pay for the food."

"It's okay," I said. "It wasn't Mikey's fault." I took the Treats to the garden hose

and washed off most of the grass. I changed
the price on the cardboard sign to:

```
Tasty Rice Krispie Treats
        50 cents  10 cents
Ice Cold Lemonade  50 cents
```

Every time someone came by, they
looked at the plate and kept walking. After a
while I had to recite the times tables, just to
keep from crying. I was on *three times seven*
when, out of nowhere, Dr. Pepper came
charging toward the table again.

I flapped my arms at him and said, "Bad
dog. Shoo. Scram." But I didn't say it too
loud because Philip told me that once Dr.
Pepper started following him home from
school, so he yelled scram. But Dr. Pepper
didn't scram. He tried to take a bite out of
Philip's rear end. I didn't dare yell loud and
get Dr. Pepper mad at me. I made sure I

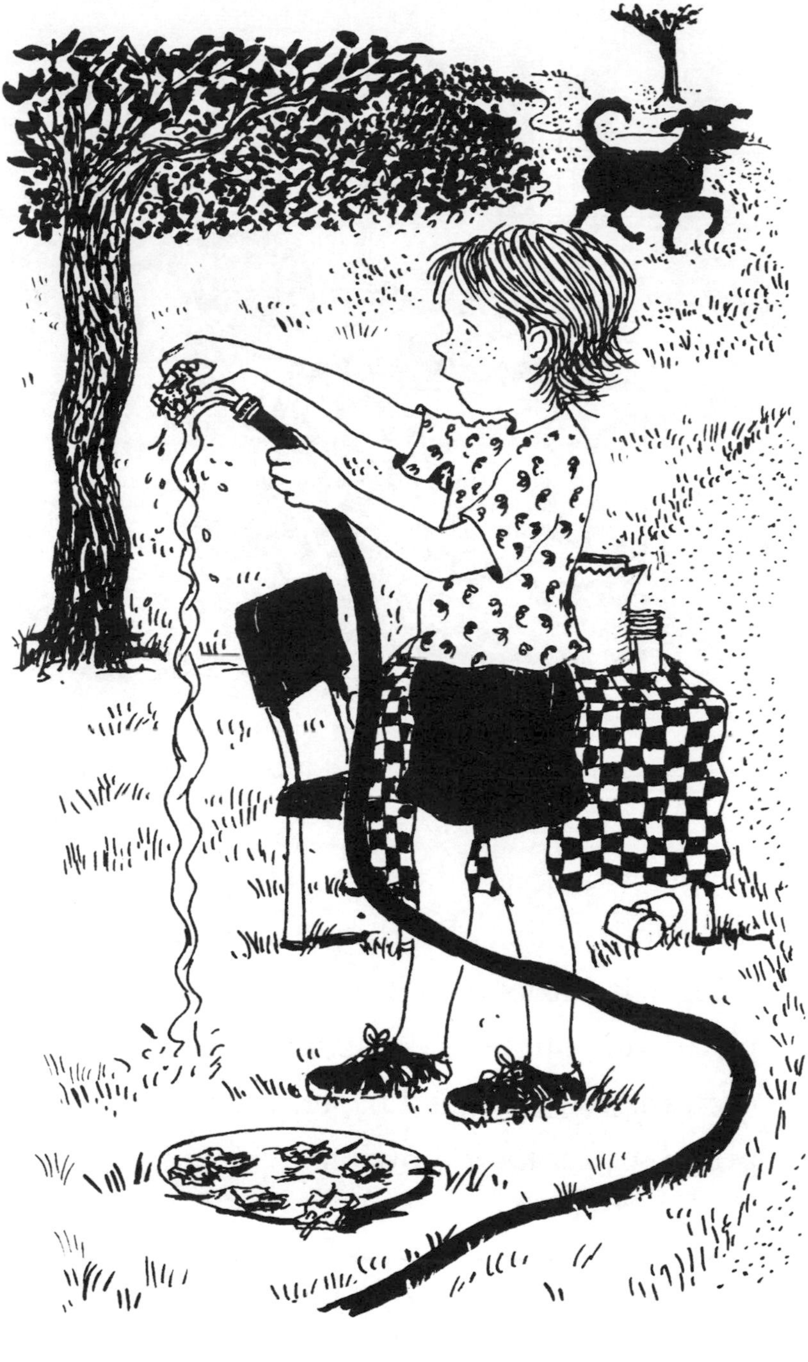

didn't stand up either; I stayed in my chair where my rear end would be safe. But Dr. Pepper wasn't afraid of me. He grabbed the tablecloth in his mouth and pulled. Everything fell and bounced off Dr. Pepper—the plate, the pitcher, the cups, the napkins, even the roll of waxed paper. He was so surprised, he took off, howling.

I looked at the mess on the ground. Now the Treats were covered with grass, plus dirt and dog drool. I threw them in the trash. I never got to put wads of money in the cigar box under the table or count it and spread the dollar bills into a fan, like I had planned to do after everything was sold.

When I went upstairs to get ready for bed that night, I tore the picture of the Skylark glasses off my bulletin board and threw it into the wastebasket. I got under the covers and cried into Jingle Bell's fur. He doesn't mind when I do that.

My mother came in, sat on my bed, and rubbed my back. "I'm sorry about what happened," she said. "You don't have to pay back the money you owe me."

"I wanted to buy the glasses so bad," I mumbled into my pillow.

"I know," said Mom.

"I have to tell Amy I can't be in the wedding," I said. "It's a known fact everyone will laugh at me if I don't give an expensive gift."

"Where did you get a ridiculous idea like that?" Mom asked. "In fact, my favorite gifts have always been things people took the time to make for me instead of buy."

"Honest?"

"Cross my heart."

"You mean like the potholders I made you for Mother's Day?" I asked.

"Exactly," said Mom.

"Do you think potholders are a dumb gift from someone in the wedding party?"

"Absolutely not. Peter and Amy would love them. I'm sure of it. And Amy's registry list shows the colors she wants in her kitchen. She wants blue and yellow."

After my mother left, I got out of bed and dug around in my closet till I found the box of loops and my potholder frame. I had a whole bag of light blue and most of a bag of bright yellow loops. I fell asleep that night, planning the patterns I would weave.

The Package

★ ★ ★
★ ★ ★

On the first day of school, every family in our district got a calendar that listed all the school events for the year. The first thing Philip did with ours was circle the important dates like: start of Thanksgiving holiday, start of Christmas break, and start of winter break. Then he gave it to me and said, "Hey, Beanhead, you should use this to count down the days till the wedding."

I looked at the calendar and saw that it was exactly ten weeks away. I started to bite my nails.

"Mom," I asked, as she was hanging the

calendar on the kitchen bulletin board, "how many people do you think will be at Amy's wedding?"

My mom put her hands on her hips and said, "You're starting to worry about the wedding, aren't you?"

"No . . . well, maybe, but just a little," I said.

"Try not to get all worked up over it, honey. You'll be a wreck by November."

So I tried not to think about it. I tried not to worry about walking down the aisle with everyone's eyes looking at me; I tried not to think about all the things that could go wrong. And I didn't, for two whole days, until Carol Ann asked me if I had my dress for the wedding yet. When I told her I'd probably wear the only party dress I have, she laughed at me. She told me I had to wear something called a flower-girl dress. She said, "When I was in a wedding, my dress was very, very fancy, almost as fancy as the bride's. My mother said the dress cost an arm and a leg, but I don't think it did. I think it cost a lot of money, though. It had a huge, crinkly slip under it that stuck out so far no one could come near me. All day long everybody told me I looked like a princess, and people took about a million pictures of me."

After school Carol Ann asked me to stop at her house to see her dress. I called my mom to let her know where I was. Then I went up to Carol Ann's room. When I saw the dress, I didn't say it out loud, but I thought it was kind of ugly. It was bright purple, the color of my purple pizzazz cosmic crayon, with ruffles everywhere. The bottom part was long and had a whole bunch of layers of lacy ruffles. The sleeves were made of lace, too. And Carol Ann was right—it stuck out a mile. It had a matching hat that looked like a Frisbee. There were lace gloves, too.

"Try it on," she said, taking the dress off the hanger. "If it fits, you can borrow it." She sounded excited. She had worn it two years ago, and it looked kind of small, so I said I'd try it on, just to show her it didn't fit.

"Hmm," Carol Ann said, when she saw that it was too tight to zip up the back. "We can fix that." She left the room. While she was gone, I scratched around my neck, where the dress itched the most. She came

back with four giant safety pins. Then she yanked and tugged and pinned the back shut. "No one will even notice the pins if you wear the gorgeous hat," she said, as she put the Frisbee on my head and tied it under my chin by its long purple ribbons. She stepped back and looked at me. "Be sure to wear tights, purple ones. The dress is just a little bit short."

"I can't breathe," I said.

Carol Ann sighed. "It doesn't matter how you feel," she said. "It's a wedding. What matters is how you look."

When I turned to the big mirror on the back of her bedroom door, I almost said "Yikes!" right out loud. I looked like the picture of Little Bo Peep in my nursery rhyme book.

"What do you think?" asked Carol Ann. "Do you want to borrow it? It doesn't look

as good on you as it did on me. But . . ."
She tugged at the bottom of the skirt to try
to make it look longer.

"Thanks, Carol Ann. But it isn't right for
me," I said. Then Carol Ann poked around
in her closet and pulled out a magazine
about weddings. "I picked my dress out
of this magazine," she said. "Maybe we can
find something for you." She turned to

all the pages that showed flower-girl dresses.

As soon as I got home, I told my mother, "Mom, I can't be in the wedding. They are going to make me wear a fancy, magazine dress and no one will come near me. Carol Ann said so."

My mother mumbled something under her breath. The only thing I could understand were the words *Carol Ann*. Then she told me that I should call Amy and talk to her about it. I'm sort of scared to call grownups on the phone, so I asked Mom if she'd do it for me.

"No, this is something you have to do yourself. You need to tell Amy how you feel and find out how she feels and come to some agreement about what you're going to wear," Mom said.

To get ready to make the phone call, I first bit my nails for a while. Then I worked

on a potholder while I planned what I
would say. Then I put Jingle Bell next to the
phone so I could look at him while I talked,
and started to dial. I got as far as the last
number before I hung up. I decided to wait
till the next day. The next day I got as far
as the phone starting to ring before I hung

up. Jingle Bell understood how hard it was.

What got me to actually finish making the call was my mother telling me that if I didn't hurry up and call, Amy might think I didn't care and might pick out a dress herself, and then it would be too late. I dialed Amy's number. When it started to ring, I got so nervous I kept whispering, "Please don't be home. Please don't be home," after each ring.

"Hello?" said Amy.

"Hi, Amy. I don't want a magazine dress for the wedding," I said, and hung up. A minute later our phone rang. It was Amy.

"Hi, Bean," she said. "I think we got cut off. I'm glad you called because I wanted to talk to you about your dress. I've finally got the bridesmaids' dresses under control and you're next on my list. Here's what I'm thinking. The bridesmaids are wearing blue, so blue might be nice for your dress, too.

And I'd like your dress to be something you'd be comfortable wearing. In fact, I'd like you to write down some ideas or draw a picture of the kind of dress you'd like. Would you do that?"

"Okay," I said. I was smiling. I was also trying to remember where I had put my big pad of drawing paper.

"And let me know what size you wear," she went on. "The seamstress who's making my dress said she'll make yours, too. When it's finished, I'll send it to you to try on. If it doesn't fit, she can fix it. If you hate it, you have to promise you'll tell me, and we can start over. Okay?"

"Okay," I said, giving Jingle Bell a thumbs-up sign.

After I hung up, Jingle Bell watched as I took out my box of sixty-four crayons with the sharpener built right into the box. I took out all the blue crayons and drew two pictures. One showed the kind of dress I do *not* want, and the other showed a dress I would like.

I also made a list.

Not like this

this is ok

THINGS I DO NOT WANT
No big skirt
No ruffles
No scrachy cloth
No slip that doesn't let people come near me and I can't go to the bathroom wearing it

Every time I put the word *No,* I made it big so that Amy wouldn't miss it. I sent everything to Amy and waited for the dress to come in the mail. Every day I ran into the house after school, yelling, "Did it come?"

If it was my mom who heard me, she always answered, "Sorry, honey, not yet."

If my brother heard me, he always answered, "No, the new brain you ordered hasn't come yet, Beanhead."

Finally, one day when I ran up the porch steps after school, I saw a big sign taped to the door. The sign said, IT CAME!!! I ran into the house. On the desk in our front hall was a box addressed to Miss Bernice Sherwin-Hendricks, Flower Girl.

Mom and Philip watched as I opened the box. In it were my flower-girl dress and a letter from Amy.

The letter said:

Dear Bean (World's Greatest
Flower Girl 🌸),
 The seamstress tried to make
the dress you drew. I hope it
fits and you like it. The lady at
the fabric store said the fabric
will not wrinkle even if you
scrunch it into a ball. I wish
my wedding dress was like that!
Remember, you promised to
tell me if there's anything
you don't like.
 Bean, I can't wait for the
Big Day. How about you?
                    Love,
                    Amy
     Excited (but nervous)
        Bride-to-be
P.S. Tell your mom the dress is
machine-washable.

I lifted the dress out of the box. It was
absolutely the most wonderful, perfect
flower-girl dress in the whole world. The

cloth was soft. It was light blue with little flowers printed all over it. Down the front were the most awesome buttons, shaped like bunnies. Each bunny even had little pink eyes. I knew my dress was more of a princess dress than Carol Ann's. I ran up to my room and tried it on. It fit, and it didn't feel scratchy, not one little bit!

Every day I put on the dress after supper and practiced walking the length of our upstairs hall, pretending it was the church aisle. One night I even slept in my flower-girl dress. I didn't mean to, though. I was wearing it in my room one night, pretending to be a princess, and my father kept yelling up the stairs, "Time for bed." Then he switched to, "Time for bed, and I mean it." Then he switched to, "If I come up there and you're not in bed, young lady, you are in very serious trouble." But I was in the middle of being locked in the mean king's tower and trying to signal with my flashlight out the tower window for the prince to come and rescue me, and I just couldn't stop. Then I heard footsteps coming up the stairs (not the tower stairs, the Sherwin-Hendricks stairs), so I jumped into bed with my dress on and pulled the covers up to my chin. It

was my dad coming to read to me and kiss
me good night. I fell asleep in the middle of
his story and didn't wake up till the next
morning. I was scared I had ruined my dress.
I ran to my dresser mirror to see how it
looked. The fabric store lady was right; it
did not have one single wrinkle in it!

I guess I talked about the dress a lot at
school because one day Carol Ann said, "Bet
your mom won't let you wear the dress to
school."

So then I had to say, "She will too."

Then Carol Ann said, "Will not," and I said, "Will too." And before I knew it I was saying that my mom is a nice mom and she lets me do anything I want.

So then Julie butted in and told me to prove it.

When I asked Mom about wearing the dress to school, she said no. My mom says no a lot. She said the dress was just too special. I told her I would not climb on the jungle gym or even swing during recess, so it wouldn't get dirty or ripped. I reminded her that Amy had said it was machine washable. I wanted to tell her about sleeping in it without it wrinkling, but I didn't. "Please, pretty please with sugar on top," I begged.

Then my mother sighed. Sighing is good. Sighing means Mom is getting tired and might give in. So I kept talking real fast and saying that it was very, very, very important for me to wear the dress to school, and she could lock me in my room and throw away the key if I didn't come home with it in perfect shape. I added a few more pretty pleases and pleases with sugar and gummy bears on top. Finally she said yes.

The next day, right after the pledge, Ms. Babbitt told the class that I had something special to share with them. She told them I wanted to show my flower-girl dress. As I was walking to the front of the room, Carol Ann raised her hand and told the class that she'd already been in a wedding and that people told her she looked like a princess. I was about to give Carol Ann a mad look for trying to spoil my dress showing when Ms. Babbitt said, "That's lovely, Carol Ann, but today we're talking about Beany's wedding experience."

Ms. Babbitt asked me to walk up and down the aisles so each student could see the bunny buttons. I felt so happy, I wanted to hug Ms. Babbitt. But I would never do that. Instead I wrote her a note. She has a little mailbox on her desk for us to write stuff to her like: Please move my seat away from Kevin Gates. He pokes me in the back and pulls my hair. After showing my dress, I wrote: You are nice. From Beany.

After lunch, Carol Ann, Julie, and I were on the playground. Carol Ann and Julie were swinging. I was standing next to the swings, keeping my dress clean. Kevin Gates and some of the other boys were playing dodge ball in the field near us. All of a sudden Kevin threw the ball right at me. It hit me in the back, and I fell into the stones around the swings. Kevin ran over to me and said, "Oh, sorry—hope I didn't ruin your

stupid dress." I was mad at Kevin, but I was
too scared of him to say anything. Kevin can
be very mean.

Carol Ann wasn't scared; she was just
mad. She took the ball and wouldn't give it
back to Kevin. "Get out of here, you big

lunkhead!" she yelled at him. Julie helped me up. We dusted the stones and dirt from the dress, but it was still pretty dirty. I had to say the times tables to keep from crying right there on the playground.

At dismissal, Kevin pushed ahead of me in line. Then he turned around and started to laugh. I was too scared of him to ask why he was laughing, but he told me. "One of your stupid buttons is missing. Now you're in trouble." My bus number was being called over the PA. I had to leave or I would miss my bus.

All the way home I sat next to Carol Ann, wiping my eyes and snuffling to keep my nose from running.

"Do you think someone will find the button and turn it in at the office?" I asked.

"Maybe," Carol Ann said. "Unless the person who finds it likes bunnies."

"Do you think if we go out on the playground tomorrow as soon as we get to school we could find it?" I asked Carol Ann.

"Maybe," she said, "but it'll probably be scrunched by then."

"I'm scared to tell my mom," I said. "I told her she could lock me in my room and throw away the key if something happened. Can I stay at your house?"

"They'd find you," Carol Ann said. "You better go home. Just don't say anything. Put the dress in the laundry and hope your mom washes it without seeing how dirty it is and hope it comes out clean and hope nobody notices that a button is missing."

"That's a lot to hope for," I said.

"Well, you're the one who wanted to wear the dress to school."

When I got home I stuffed the dress

down to the bottom of the laundry hamper in the bathroom, then went right to my room and lay on my bed, hugging Jingle Bell. At supper I sat with my eyes down so no one would see that they were puffy from crying. But my mom saw. She asked what was wrong. I said, "Nothing."

She said, "Come on. Something's wrong."

"I don't want to talk about it."

"You'll feel better if you do," she said.

"I don't want to talk about it," I said again. So, for the rest of the meal, I pushed the food around on my plate while Dad talked about how we leave too many lights turned on and do we think money grows on trees and are we trying to make the electric company rich. When everyone got up to put their plates in the sink, I blurted out, "Mom, I guess you'll have to lock me in my room and throw away the key."

My brother said, "Cool!"

My mother put down her plate and said, "Oh dear, does that mean what I think it means?"

My dad said, "What, may I ask, is going on?"

I told them about Kevin being a lunkhead. "It was a dumb idea to wear the dress to school."

My mom got the dress out of the hamper and sprayed some stuff on it that gets stains out. Then she put it in the washing machine. While the machine sloshed and slooshed, trying to get my dress clean, Dad took his car keys off the hook on the kitchen wall. He took flashlights out of the drawer next to the sink. "Let's go," he said.

The four of us and Jingle Bell drove to the school playground. It was dark. Dad aimed the flashlights onto the ground by the swing set while Mom, Philip, and I bent our heads close to the ground, searching for the bunny button. I tried to keep my eyes open as wide as they would go and not blink, so I wouldn't miss seeing it. I crossed my fingers on both hands for luck. I kept whispering, "Please be here, please be here."

Philip was the one who first saw something

in the grass. "Dad, aim the flashlight here, near my foot," he said. And there it was, dirty and covered with grass—my button. It wasn't even scrunched.

Dad smiled and hugged me. Mom spit on a tissue and cleaned off the button. Philip said, "Does this mean we don't get to lock you in your room and throw away the key?" I knew he was joking though because he punched me on the arm after he said it.

When we got home Mom and I ran down to the basement to get my dress out of the washing machine. "Please be clean," I whispered as Mom lifted it out. The dress was beautiful. When it was dry Mom sewed the button back on, put the dress on a hanger with a plastic bag over it, and hung it in my closet. I looked at it every day. Sometimes I reached inside the plastic bag and rubbed my fingers over the buttons, they were so smooth. But I didn't wear the dress again, no matter how much I wanted to, till the wedding.

The Rehearsal

★ ★ ★
★ ★ ★

On the last day of school before the wedding I was so nervous I missed three math facts on our weekly test, and once, when Ms. Babbitt called on me to read, I didn't know the place. At recess she asked me if anything was wrong. I told her I was trying to pay attention to her, but my brain kept thinking about the wedding.

"Well, you be sure to enjoy yourself," said Ms. Babbitt. I told her I'd try.

On the bus ride home Carol Ann gave me a bunch of last-minute instructions. "Whatever you do, don't catch the bride's bouquet when she throws it at all the girls who aren't married," she warned. "Catching it means you'll be the next one to get married whether you want to or not." That scared me. Then she asked me if I was going to throw flower petals out of a basket as I walked down the church aisle. I told her I didn't know yet. I'd find out at the rehearsal that night.

"Well, in case you do, let me give you some advice," she said. "Don't run out of flower petals before you run out of aisle. When my sister Margo was a flower girl, that happened to her. She was throwing big handfuls of flower petals, and then halfway down the aisle she ran out. She had to scratch around at the bottom of her basket and start throwing bits of leaves and junk. I can't believe people didn't laugh at her right out loud. If I invite you to be in my Flower

Girl Club, I'll bring pictures of it to a meeting. They're so funny. And another thing, my mom said that she was a bridesmaid once and you know how they unroll a big piece of white paper down the middle aisle of the church and everyone in the wedding walks on it? Well, my mom's heel kept ripping the paper, and it was full of holes by the time the bride walked on it. So don't drag your feet

like you always do. And one more thing, it is a known fact . . ."

"Carol Ann," I cut in, before she could tell me anything else that might go wrong, "I don't want to talk about weddings anymore." Carol Ann got sort of hurt. She took out her science book and studied the planets for the rest of the ride home.

My family didn't eat supper that night. We just ate toasted English muffins with butter and jelly, because there was going to be an eating party after the rehearsal. We put our wedding presents into the car to give to Amy and Peter at the party. I had made fourteen potholders and wrapped them in silver paper with white bells all over it. Philip asked if he could put his name on the wedding card I had made, so it would look like they were from him, too, but I said, "No way!"

Amy had told us not to dress up for the rehearsal so I wore jeans, but I wore my wedding shoes to get used to walking down the aisle in them. I found the shoes on a sale rack at Sears and knew they were perfect. They were sparkly and glittery. At first, my mother didn't want to buy them. She called them gaudy. I think that means ugly. But I told her they made me feel like Dorothy in *The Wizard of Oz*, so she said okay.

At the rehearsal, a girl named Dallas was in charge. Amy's parents hired her to make sure everything in the wedding happened the right way. Dallas stood at the back of the church and told everybody what to do. Reverend Callan also told everybody what to do, but he smiled a lot more than Dallas. I found out that I was supposed to throw petals from a basket, just like Carol Ann had said. But I had another job, too. Under the petals was a shiny white pillow. The bride and groom's rings were tied to it with ribbons. During the wedding I was supposed to go up to Reverend Callan when he said, "The rings, please." Then he would untie them and take them. He told me that being in charge of the rings was a very important job. I didn't want an important job. I looked at the rings, tied with white ribbons. I knew I had to guard them with my life till the wedding. I put the basket handle over my arm and decided not to take it off till I got back home.

Then we did a pretend wedding. I didn't think I would be too nervous for the pretend wedding because hardly any people were there, but when it was my turn to go down the aisle my legs got all bobbly and wobbly. I remembered what Carol Ann had

said about her mom ripping the paper, so I
tried to lift my feet real high as I walked.
When I was halfway to the altar, Dallas
yelled out, "Stop the show!" Then she told
me to start over and flow down the aisle.
While I flowed, I tried to count how many

steps it took to get to the front. I figured that might help me get through it the next day. Like when the doctor is giving me a shot she says, "By the time you count to five the shot will be over." The problem with the church was that I had to count all the way to thirty-eight before I got to the front. When I was done, Dallas told me, "This is not a fifty-yard dash. Tomorrow, take it slower. People will want to look at you." I started to bite my nails.

After we finished practicing, I went up to Reverend Callan and tapped his arm. "What do we do if we have to go to the bathroom during the wedding?" I asked him.

"That's a very good question," he said. "I used to wonder about that myself when I first started out in this business. But I have learned that the best solution is to go to the bathroom last thing, just before the service. I always do that. There's a bathroom at the back of the church."

Dallas told all of us to get a good night's sleep and be bright and ready for W Day, which meant wedding day. Then we went downstairs to the church hall for the rehearsal party. Besides the people from the rehearsal, anyone who had traveled from another city to come to the wedding was invited.

Each place at the dinner tables had a little card telling who should sit there. My scat was next to Peter's. I wished I could sit with Philip and my mother and father. With them I wouldn't have to talk if I didn't feel like it. But Peter would probably ask me, "How's school?" and ask how old I was and stuff like that. And I would get tired trying to smile and not spill anything and not say anything dumb.

Amy was on Peter's other side. She said

she'd arranged it that way so Peter would be between the two most gorgeous girls in the whole place. "You are surrounded by beauty," she told him.

"I'm surrounded by freckles," Peter answered. "Help! I'm getting dizzy. I'm seeing spots in front of my eyes."

Amy didn't even mind that he made fun

of her freckles. She just laughed and told him it was our fantastic good looks that were making him dizzy. Then she kissed him, with me sitting right there watching.

"Isn't she awful?" Peter said to me. "She adores me so much. She spotted me one day in law school and started to follow me around like a puppy. I finally felt sorry for the poor thing and decided to marry her. Are you married?"

I giggled.

"Marriage is no laughing matter," he said. "Especially marriage to your cousin, Amy. Did you know she can't cook?"

"She makes good chocolate chip cookies," I told him.

"Well, that settles it. I was thinking of changing my mind about marrying her, but now I will definitely show up tomorrow morning at eleven."

"I think the wedding is at ten o'clock," I corrected him.

Amy leaned over him and said, "Bean, he's just pulling your leg. He'll show up at ten, if he knows what's good for him." She kissed him again.

While we ate dinner, Peter said he heard about me going to camp for the first time and congratulated me for surviving. Then he told me stories about the first time he went to camp. I told him about the scary noises under my cabin. He told me his three favorite flavors of ice cream. I told him I knew how to spell *deodorant.*

I had a good time at dinner, except I had a hard time eating because of the basket on my arm. I could not cut my chicken or put butter on my roll.

After the meal Amy and Peter gave out presents. They gave all the men who were in the wedding gold key rings with their initials on them. They gave the bridesmaids pearl necklaces to wear the next day. Then came my turn. I was hoping I wouldn't get a key ring because I already have one with a plastic Daisy Duck on it. And I was hoping I wouldn't get pearls because they were kind of small, and I already had a necklace with four big strands of pink pearls on it that I got at a garage sale for fifty cents.

When my turn came to unwrap my gift, Peter offered to hold my basket, but I told him no because I was guarding it with my life. The gift was a pen with my initials, BSH, carved on it in gold. The pen was in a blue fuzzy box. Peter told me the pen had been invented when the astronauts went into space. It would write even if it was held upside down.

"Did you pick this out?" I asked Peter.

"Yeah."

"I like it," I told him. "Thank you."

"I'm glad we got to sit together for dinner," he said. "I can see why Amy thinks you're special." He put his arm around my shoulder and squeezed it.

Amy leaned over and said to me, "Hey,

are you trying to steal my boyfriend?"

I knew she was kidding because she winked after she said it, but still, my face got all red.

After dinner Philip and I sat at a table trying to write upside down on a napkin with my new pen. I had trouble because of the basket, but Philip wrote out his whole name. I knew Philip liked the pen because he said, "I'll buy it off you." But I wouldn't sell it, not for a million dollars. Every few minutes relatives that we hardly knew stopped at our table to kiss us and tell us how big we were getting. Then my Uncle John came over to ask if I remembered how to do the chicken dance. Aunt Florence sat down and showed us the bumpy blue veins on her legs. She called them very close veins and told us she was getting an operation on them.

Finally, Philip said to me, "Let's get out of

here." I put my pen back into its blue fuzzy box, put the box into my basket and followed him.

When he went up to the church and started to climb the stairs to the choir loft, I whispered, "We better not. We'll get in trouble." But Philip said he wanted to see what it looked like in the choir loft and kept going. I didn't want to be left alone in the dark church, so I followed. I almost tripped in my *Wizard of Oz* shoes, trying to keep up with him on the narrow stairway.

It was dark and shadowy in the choir loft. Philip sat down at the organ and spread his fingers over the keyboard.

"I'm the phantom of the opera," he said, and waved his hands up and down over the keys. I was scared, but it was kind of funny. So I sat down next to him and did it, too, only my basket kept getting in the way.

"What's with you? Are you glued to that basket handle?" he asked.

"No, I'm just guarding the rings with my life."

"The rings are in there? They're trusting you with the rings?"

"Well, I *am* the ring bearer."

"Let's see." Philip poked around in the basket and untied one of the rings. "This isn't a real wedding ring. It's fake," he said. He bent the ring into an oval instead of a circle. "This is a cheap ring, just for decoration. No way would Peter let you have the real rings ahead of time."

"Let's see," I said. I took the ring and squeezed it. It bent even more.

"You're right, it's fake," I said. All night I'd been guarding dumb fake rings with my life. I missed out on a buttered roll because of them. My arm was red because of them.

But now I could relax. I wouldn't have to worry about rings till the next day.

I sat down at the keyboard and finally took the basket off my arm. I pretended to play "Here Comes the Bride" on the organ. I raised my hands up and down over the keys and dum-dum-dee-dummed the song.

"This organ is awesome," Philip said. It was made of shiny dark wood, with rows of knobs above the keyboard and a long row of narrow wooden slats under the bench. Philip touched the slats lightly with his feet. "I wonder what these boards are for, and all these knobs above the keyboard."

"Yeah, I bet it takes a million years to learn how to play," I said.

Philip started to pull some of the knobs outward, then push them back in. I was about to tell him not to do that, but before I could get the words out, one of the knobs fell off and rolled under the slats at his feet.

"Stay calm," warned my brother, when he heard me gasp. We poked our fingers between the boards, but we couldn't reach the knob. I tried blowing between the boards, hoping I could blow the knob out. That only made me dizzy. Philip tried poking my astronaut pen down between the

boards. I was so scared I let him use it. But it didn't reach.

"Philip, what if you broke the organ?" I asked. "What if it won't play "Here Comes the Bride" right? What if we ruined the whole wedding? What if we have to pay out of our allowance to get the organ fixed? What if it costs a lot and we end up paying till we're grown up, and I won't be able to get the collector Barbie I've been saving for?" I asked.

"Calm down," Philip said again. "And I'm warning you, don't cry."

Then he started to rub his ear. Philip only rubs his ear when he's very worried. I started to cry.

"Oh, great," Philip said. "That's a big help."

"I'm sorry," I said, sniffling and trying to hold my crying inside. I didn't want Philip to be mad at me.

"We have two choices," said Philip as he

rubbed his ear. "We can find the organist at
the party and tell him what happened. Or we
can just go back downstairs and not say anything. What'll it be?"

"I'm scared," I said.

"No kidding," answered Philip. "But that
is not one of the choices. Come on, what do
you want to do?"

"I want to disappear."

"That is not a choice either, Beanhead. Now, come on, help me out here." He sounded so mad, I started to cry even harder. Philip sighed. Then he put his arm around me. "I'm sorry," he said. "It's just that I'm a little scared, too."

We decided that we had to tell the organist. Philip told me he would do the talking. I thought that was a good idea. Philip is very good at talking.

We found Mr. Halligan, the organist, in the church hall talking with Reverend Callan. Philip went up to him and asked if they could talk in private.

"What's up?" asked Mr. Halligan.

"That's quite an organ you've got in the choir loft," Philip said. "A real beauty." Philip's voice sounded funny—a lot higher than it usually is.

"Yes, indeedy-do," answered Mr. Halligan, smiling. "It's a masterpiece." I gulped when he said that.

"I bet you take good care of it," said Philip, rubbing his ear.

"Yes, indeedy-do. I treat it like a baby." When Mr. Halligan said that, my hands started to feel sweaty.

"It must be hard to play, with all those knobs and foot pedals," Philip went on.

"Yes, indeedy-do," said the organist. "It's

a complicated piece of machinery." I wiped my hands down the sides of my jeans. I wished Mr. Halligan would stop smiling. "I was wondering if we could go up to the choir loft for a minute," said Philip. "There's something I want to show you."

When we got upstairs, Mr. Halligan asked Philip what he wanted to show him.

"Well, uh, it's about the organ," stammered my brother. Mr. Halligan walked over to the organ. "What's this?" he asked when he saw the flower-girl basket on the bench.

"Oh, that's mine," I said.

"How did it get here? No one is allowed up here unless I'm present." He wasn't smiling anymore. He wasn't saying "yes, indeedy-do." He sounded mad, and we hadn't even told him yet what we had done to his organ.

I grabbed the basket so fast it fell, right onto the boards under the bench. Mr. Halligan reached down to get it. That's when he saw the knob.

"Darn," he mumbled to himself. "Did one of those knobs come loose again? I've got to get them tightened before I lose one for good." He turned to us. "I'm afraid I'm going to have to ask you to leave," he said.

"I'm very disappointed in you for coming up here without permission." He went to a cupboard in the corner of the choir loft and came back with a yardstick. He crouched down and started to swing it around under the boards till the knob came flying out. He pushed it into its hole, sat down, and started to play.

Philip and I backed out of the choir loft and ran down the stairs as fast as we could. When we got to the bottom step, we sat down. I was still shaking from being so scared.

"That was a close one," Philip said. Then he put his hand on my knee. "I'm sorry I got mad at you, Beany," he said.

"That's okay."

"And you know something? You're going to do a great job tomorrow."

"I'll be scared," I said.

"If you get scared coming down the aisle, just look at me, okay?"

"Okay," I said. We sat on the bottom step for a while, listening to the organ music. Then Philip punched me on the arm and we went back to the party.

That night I couldn't get to sleep. I thought about running out of flower petals before I ran out of aisle and about ripping holes in the white paper on the church aisle. I worried that my legs wouldn't work when the time came to walk down the aisle, or I would trip. Thirty-eight is a lot of steps to take in front of a church full of people.

Sometimes rubbing Jingle Bell's ear on my cheek helps me fall asleep. I tried it and it worked. The next thing I knew it was W Day.

The Big Day

★ ★ ★
★ ★ ★

When I woke up on W Day, I was so nervous I felt like there was a rock inside my stomach. I didn't want to eat, but my dad told me to force down something so I wouldn't feel like fainting in church. I tried to eat a bowl of cereal.

Then I put on my flower-girl dress and my *Wizard of Oz* shoes. My mother did my hair with a blow dryer and a big round brush, so it wouldn't be lumpy. Sometimes it hurt when she pulled on the brush, but I didn't say "ooch" or "ouch." It was worth the hurting to have my hair look good. She put a crown of little white flowers in my hair by jabbing hair pins all over my head. That hurt, too, but my mom said it couldn't be helped. She didn't want the flowers to fall over my eyes while I walked down the aisle. The minute she mentioned walking down the aisle my heart started to beat fast.

When we got to the church, Amy was in the dressing room at the back of the church, putting on eye shadow in front of a big mirror. "I've got to get it just right," she was mumbling to herself, "not too much, 'cause it's church, but not too little 'cause it's my wedding day." She looked so beautiful! I walked up to her and touched her dress. It felt cool and slippery. The skirt part was fluffy and made a swishing sound when she moved. As her mother helped her put on her veil, I tried to stay close to Amy so her dress would swish across my arm.

"How do I look, Bean?" she asked me.

"You look like Cinderella when she married the prince," I said.

"I feel like Cinderella," she said, and kissed my cheek. She smelled like our kitchen does when my mother picks flowers from the garden and puts them in a vase on the table.

In a couple of minutes all the bridesmaids, Peter's mother, Amy's mother, and Dallas were in the room, and it got very noisy. They all seemed to be talking at once, saying stuff like, "Help! My hairdo looks like a huge bird's nest," and "Okay, who took my left shoe?" and "I have three words to say to all of you: relax, relax, relax." (That was Dallas.)

The closer it got to the time when we would have to get in line, the more scared I felt. My hands got all wet from sweat; then I started to feel cold; then I started to shake all over. I had to leave Amy's side and sit down.

When Dallas yelled out "Five minutes!" I knew I couldn't do it. Last summer, when I told Amy I'd be in her wedding, I thought I could be the best flower girl in the whole world. But now that it was time, I just

couldn't do it. I went up to Amy and tapped her arm. "Amy," I said. "I don't want to mess up your wedding, but I have a problem. My legs aren't working right. Can you walk down the aisle without flower petals?"

Amy stooped down in front of me. Her gown fluffed out around her like a cloud. She took my hands. "Bean, I know it's scary.

I'm shaking inside, too. But we can't let being afraid stop us from doing things. Otherwise we'd miss out on so much great stuff. I was afraid to go to New York to live. But just think, if I hadn't gone I never would have met my hunk-a-love. I want you and me and everyone to enjoy this day so much. But the first thing we have to do, no matter how scared we are, is get to the altar.

"So I want you to do this. When you start walking, just think about me walking ten steps behind you. I'll be wondering if I'm going to trip, just like you. My legs will be shaky, just like yours. But I'll be watching you ahead of me. You'll keep me going. I need my Bean ahead of me so I can make it down the aisle. It's not the flower petals I need; it's you."

Amy put her arms around me and held me so tight I could feel her heart thump-

thumping. She didn't even care if it wrinkled her gown or messed up her veil.

Standing there with Amy's arms around me and her veil scratching my face, I thought about all the stuff she's done for me—like the summer I had chickenpox and was sick in bed for more than a week. That summer Amy worked during the day as an ice cream scooper at Friendly's, and every

night when I was sick she came to visit me. She brought me a different flavor ice cream sundae cup each night and read *Mr. Popper's Penguins* to me. The only time I didn't feel like scratching was when Amy read to me.

I thought about caramel popcorn and Dr. Seuss and Ladies' Day at Crystal Lake Amusement Park. I thought about how she calls me every birthday and says, "Bean, I'm so glad you were born."

Amy unwrapped her arms from me and took my face in her hands. "Can you do it?" she asked. I couldn't talk right then; my heart was so filled up with love for her, so I just shook my head yes.

"Okay, world's greatest flower girl, let's go out there and get me married."

When the organ music started, Dallas told everyone to line up. I used the bathroom, then got in my place, right ahead of Amy. Dallas told every person when they should start down the aisle. She told the first bridesmaid, "Smile, you're at a wedding, not a funeral."

She told the second bridesmaid, "Take a deep breath in through your nose and out through your mouth."

She told the third one, "Relax your shoulders. You'll be fine."

She told the fourth one, "Posture."

When it was my turn she said, "Remember, flow down the aisle." I turned around and looked at Amy. She was smiling at me. She blew me a kiss.

Dallas took my shoulders and gave me a little push through the door toward the huge bunch of people filling the pews. I spotted my mom and dad. They were smiling at me.

I looked at Philip. He put his thumbs in his ears and made a face. I almost laughed. As I walked down the aisle, I thought about Amy, ten steps behind me, watching the back of my head to keep her going.

I tried to flow, like Dallas told me. I tried not to drag my feet, like Carol Ann told me. I tried to enjoy it, like Ms. Babbitt told me.

To make sure I wouldn't run out of flower petals before I ran out of aisle, I threw just one petal at a time. I threw one petal straight in front of me, then one to the right, then one to the left. I did that over and over, slowly and carefully, till I got to the front of the church. I did it for Amy.

When I was almost at the end of the aisle, I saw that my basket still had a lot of petals in it. I needed to get rid of them so Reverend Callan could find the rings on the pillow underneath. Right before I went up the

three steps to the altar I turned the basket over and dumped out the rest of the petals. They made kind of a big pile, but Amy and her dad didn't mind; they stepped over them.

Everything went perfectly. Amy and I both made it to the altar.

After that the whole day went just right. I was smiling each time the photographer clicked his camera for the pictures of the wedding party. I ate dinner without drooling or dribbling any food. My Uncle John helped me get through the chicken dance. Best of all, before Amy and Peter left to go on their honeymoon, Peter told me I looked like a princess. It was the most perfect day of my whole life.

When I got into the car after the wedding, my lap was full. I had my basket with the shiny pillow, my flower crown, a wedding napkin that had two hearts on it, and a few spare bottles of bubbles that we all blew at Amy and Peter when they came out of church. If I joined Carol Ann's Flower Girl Club, I would show all those things at a meeting. And I would tell how I hid in the bathroom when they announced that the bride was going to throw her bouquet. I wanted to make sure it didn't land on me.

But I knew I didn't have the right words to ever tell about the important parts of the wedding, like how it felt to have my picture taken standing with Amy and Peter at the church, or how proud I was when I handed Reverend Callan the rings I'd been guarding. Even if I tried for a million years I could never tell how it felt walking down the aisle ten steps ahead of Amy, helping her make it to the altar. Those things would stay inside my heart forever.

As we pulled out of the church parking lot, my dad yelled out, "Who's the best flower girl in the world?" Mom, Dad, and Philip all answered, "Beany!" Then Philip added, quietly in my ear, "Yes, indeedy-do."

I leaned my head against his arm and fell asleep.